MW00891330

This book was given with love

To_____

From_____

Copyright © 2021 by Puppy Dogs & Ice Cream, Inc.

All rights reserved. Published in the United States
by Puppy Dogs & Ice Cream, Inc.

ISBN: 978-1-955151-38-2

Edition: September 2021

PDIC and Puppy Dogs & Ice Cream are trademarks of
Puppy Dogs & Ice Cream, Inc.

For all inquiries, please contact us at:
info@puppysmiles.org

To see more of our books, visit us at:
www.PuppyDogsAndIceCream.com

About the Author Amy Nicholson, LCPC

 As a children's therapist, I field a lot of questions by parents about typical developmental behavior in children and how to find healthy ways to encourage and discourage certain behaviors. I find that it is much more meaningful to a child when they can learn through experience rather than being simply told by a grown up. I am often asked by parents how to address these pretty typical childhood behaviors. Parents are eager to find resources to help their children navigate these life lessons and sometimes embarrassing moments!

Nosy Norris teaches a valuable life lesson about healthy social behavior woven neatly into a fun and colorful story. With illustrations that pop off the page with color and emotional expression, Nosy Norris is a helpful tool for parents to broach this ever-present topic and experience. Children, as well as parents, will be delighted by the rhyming words and humor within Norris' experiences. This book provides a healthy, helpful and fun way to learn and to talk with your child about pointing and staring.

Little Norris Nedd was nosy.
He really loved to stare.
It was a very rude habit,
but he was unaware.

He would always stop and point,
and use his eyes to gawk.
He'd scan the room from left to right,
watching people like a hawk.

Norris Nedd would always stare,
and point his little finger.
Then he'd stand so very still,
and let his long gaze linger.

He'd stare at his sister Nellie,
and his brother Noah too.
He'd just stare at everyone,
like animals in a zoo.

"Oh Norris, please stop staring,"
his mom, Nadine, would say.
"Noah never does it,
you must not act this way."

But he pretended not to hear
and just stared even more.
He loved to watch and point at things,
and thought behaving was a bore!

His mother told him it was rude,
to always point and stare.
But Norris didn't listen,
he just didn't seem to care!

He'd stare at all his classmates,
his friends and teachers too.
He just couldn't see things,
from his mother's point of view.

When he stared,
his mind would wander
far off to another place.

His face would go
completely blank
like he was up in outer space!

"Earth to Norris!" said his dad Nick,
his voice now sounding furious.
"Pay attention, are you there?
It's not good to be this curious!"

Can't you see how rude it is
to stare at all in sight?
You make us all so nervous,
and it's simply not polite!"

"Your dad is right," his mom agreed.
"It's really quite uncouth.
But I know that in due time,
you'll stumble on the truth."

And then one day, his mom was right.
While Norris ogled with his eyes,
he wasn't watching where he stepped,
and got a sticky surprise!

He was walking by a park,
with people for him to view.
He was staring so intensely
he didn't see the bright green goo.

Norris slipped and fell right down,
hitting the ground with quite a PLOP!
If he hadn't been so nosy,
he might have seen the icky slop.

Norris screamed and cried and wailed,
and all the children turned to see.
Now they were the ones staring,
and they began to laugh with glee.

They all laughed and pointed
when he fell and went kaput.
Staring wasn't so funny,
with the shoe on the other foot!

His father helped him up,
and put him back on his two feet.
They walked back to their house,
trailing slime all down the street.

His mother helped to clean him up,
while Norris sat in a chair.
He cried out to his parents,
"I'll never stare again, I swear!"

And ever since that fateful day,
Norris didn't stare.
He always watched his step,
and walked around with care.

Norris quit being nosy,
and stopped pointing all the time.
He always kept an eye out
for sticky, bright green slime!

Claim your FREE Gift!

 Visit:

PDICBooks.com/Gift

Thank you for purchasing

and welcome to the Puppy Dogs & Ice Cream family.
We're certain you're going to love the little gift
we've prepared for you at the website above.